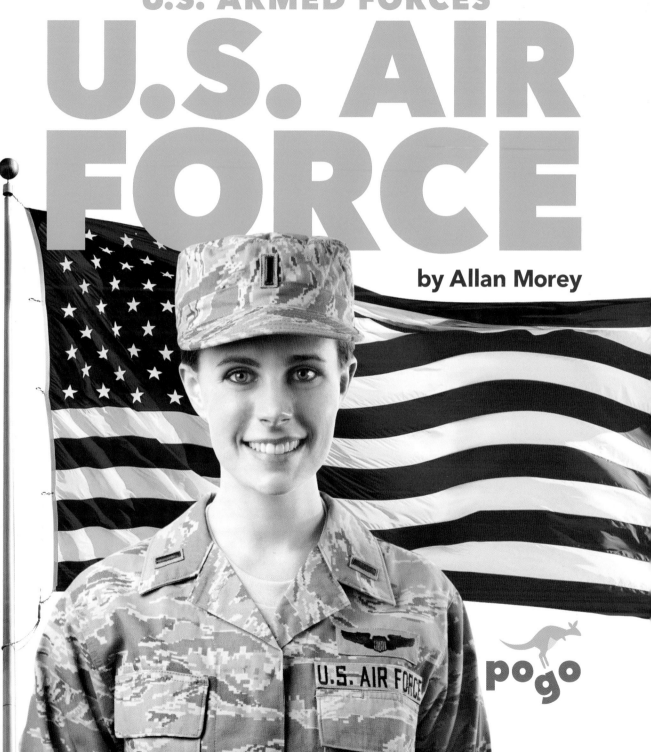

U.S. ARMED FORCES

U.S. AIR FORCE

by Allan Morey

pogo

Ideas for Parents and Teachers

Pogo Books let children practice reading informational text while introducing them to nonfiction features such as headings, labels, sidebars, maps, and diagrams, as well as a table of contents, glossary, and index.

Carefully leveled text with a strong photo match offers early fluent readers the support they need to succeed.

Before Reading

- "Walk" through the book and point out the various nonfiction features. Ask the student what purpose each feature serves.
- Look at the glossary together. Read and discuss the words.

Read the Book

- Have the child read the book independently.
- Invite him or her to list questions that arise from reading.

After Reading

- Discuss the child's questions. Talk about how he or she might find answers to those questions.
- Prompt the child to think more. Ask: Before reading this book, did you know what types of jobs U.S. Air Force members perform? What more would you like to learn about the U.S. Air Force?

Pogo Books are published by Jump!
5357 Penn Avenue South
Minneapolis, MN 55419
www.jumplibrary.com

Library of Congress Cataloging-in-Publication Data

Names: Morey, Allan, author.
Title: U.S. Air Force / by Allan Morey.
Description: Minneapolis, MN: Jump!, [2021]
Series: U.S. Armed Forces
Audience: Ages 7-10 | Audience: Grades 2-3
Identifiers: LCCN 2019049847 (print)
LCCN 2019049848 (ebook)
ISBN 9781645274193 (hardcover)
ISBN 9781645274209 (ebook)
Subjects: LCSH: United States. Air Force—Juvenile literature. | Airmen—United States—Juvenile literature.
Classification: LCC UG633 .M59 2021 (print)
LCC UG633 (ebook) | DDC 358.400973—dc23
LC record available at https://lccn.loc.gov/2019049847
LC ebook record available at https://lccn.loc.gov/2019049848

Editor: Susanne Bushman
Designer: Molly Ballanger

Content Consultant: Captain Cody Morgan, Pilot, United States Air Force

At the time of print, Captain Cody Morgan had been in the U.S. Air Force for six years. He started out in pilot training in Texas and stayed as a T-6 Texan Instructor Pilot. He is currently stationed at Travis Air Force Base, California, where he flies the C-5M Super Galaxy. It is the largest airplane in the U.S. Air Force!

Photo Credits: Eliyahu Yosef Parypa/Shutterstock, cover; DanielBendjy/iStock, 1 (foreground); turtix/Shutterstock, 1 (background); U.S. Air Force, 3, 5, 6-7tl, 6-7tr, 6-7br, 8, 9, 10-11, 12-13, 14-15, 17, 20-21, 23; Andrew_Howe/iStock, 4; Bruce Leibowitz/Shutterstock, 6-7bl; Fasttailwind/Shutterstock, 16; RP Library/Alamy, 18-19.

Printed in the United States of America at Corporate Graphics in North Mankato, Minnesota.

TABLE OF CONTENTS

CHAPTER 1

IN THE AIR

A jet zooms overhead. It is a U.S. Air Force fighter jet! It is on **patrol**. It looks for danger.

fighter jet

The Air Force is part of the U.S. military. Its members are called Airmen. They **defend** the United States. They fight in the air and in space. They even work in **cyberspace**! They also protect U.S. **allies**.

bomber

gunship

fighter jet

C-5M Super Galaxy

The Air Force uses many **aircraft**. Large bombers drop bombs. Gunships shoot from the sky. Fighter jets attack enemy airplanes. The C-5M Super Galaxy carries supplies. It is the Air Force's largest airplane!

WHAT DO YOU THINK?

Drones are special aircraft. Why? They are flown **remotely**. They can carry weapons. They can be used to spy on enemies, too. Would you like to control a drone?

CHAPTER 2

AIR FORCE JOBS

Recruits go through Basic Training. They learn about serving in the Air Force. They learn to fire weapons. They are tested physically.

Next, Airmen go to school. Why? They train for jobs. Then most are sent to a **base**. They will work there. They will live there, too!

Airmen do many jobs. Some are mechanics. Others work in health care. Some are air traffic controllers. They guide aircraft as they land and take off.

DID YOU KNOW?

Many **NASA** astronauts have served in the Air Force. This includes Buzz Aldrin. He was one of the first people to land on the moon. He was an Air Force pilot.

air traffic controller ······▶

Airmen with college degrees can become officers. They go to Officer Training School. They learn important roles. Some take charge during **combat**. Others lead rescue **missions**. Some officers become doctors!

TAKE A LOOK!

Officers have different **ranks**. They show them on their uniforms. **Insignia** go on both shoulders. Take a look!

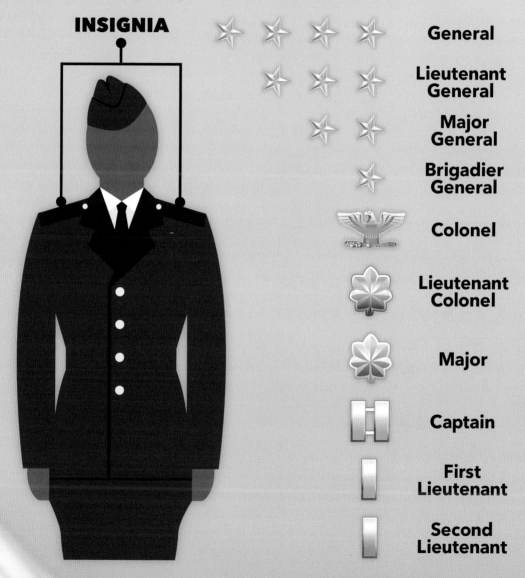

INSIGNIA

General

Lieutenant General

Major General

Brigadier General

Colonel

Lieutenant Colonel

Major

Captain

First Lieutenant

Second Lieutenant

tanker

Air Force pilots must be officers. Some fly bombers and fighter jets. Others fly helicopters. Some are tanker pilots. Tankers **refuel** other aircraft. They do this in the air!

DID YOU KNOW?

The Thunderbirds is a special group. These Air Force pilots tour the world. Why? They show their flying skills.

CHAPTER 3

AIR FORCE MISSIONS

During war, the Air Force flies combat missions. Fighter jets shoot down enemy planes. Bombers strike enemy targets.

fighter jet

bomber

The Air Force also helps other military **branches**. Airmen **transport** soldiers. They fly airdrops. What are these? Airmen drop supplies. They parachute to the ground.

supplies ·····▶

The Air Force helps during **natural disasters**. In 2010, an earthquake hit Haiti. Airmen flew to the area. They fixed the country's airport. They helped people, too. How? They brought food, water, and medicine.

WHAT DO YOU THINK?

The U.S. president is the Commander in Chief. What does this mean? He or she decides how to use the U.S. military. Would you like to do this job? Why or why not?

Some Airmen train for rescue missions. They save people who are in danger. They have medical training. They can help people who are hurt.

Air Force members protect people around the world. Would you like to serve in the U.S. Air Force?

QUICK FACTS & TOOLS

TIMELINE

1907
The U.S. Army establishes an Aeronautical Division to research the use of flying machines, like hot air balloons and airplanes.

1913
The 1st Reconnaissance Squadron becomes the Army's first air combat unit.

2019
On December 20, the Space Force, a military branch under the Air Force, is signed into law.

1947
The Air Force becomes its own U.S. military branch.

1953
The U.S. Air Force Thunderbirds Squadron is formed.

U.S. AIR FORCE MISSION
The mission of the U.S. Air Force is to fly, fight, and win in air, space, and cyberspace.

U.S. AIR FORCE ACTIVE DUTY MEMBERS:
around 328,000 (as of 2019)
Active duty members serve full-time.

U.S. AIR FORCE RESERVE MEMBERS:
around 69,000 (as of 2019)
Reserve members train and serve part-time.

aircraft: Vehicles that can fly.

allies: Countries that are on the same side during wars or military actions.

base: A permanent military station.

branches: The groups of the U.S. military, including the U.S. Air Force, U.S. Army, U.S. Coast Guard, U.S. Marine Corps, and U.S. Navy.

combat: Fighting.

cyberspace: The world of communication and interaction represented by the internet.

defend: To protect.

insignia: Symbols that show the ranks of people in the military.

missions: Tasks or jobs.

NASA: Short for National Aeronautics and Space Administration; the government agency responsible for space exploration and research.

natural disasters: Events in nature, such as hurricanes, earthquakes, and floods, that cause a lot of damage.

patrol: To keep watch over an area.

ranks: Positions in the military.

recruits: New members of a military force.

refuel: To supply more fuel.

remotely: In a remote, or faraway, location.

transport: To carry from place to place.

INDEX

TO LEARN MORE

Finding more information is as easy as 1, 2, 3.

① Go to www.factsurfer.com

② Enter "U.S.AirForce" into the search box.

③ Click the "Surf" button to see a list of websites.

FACT SURFER